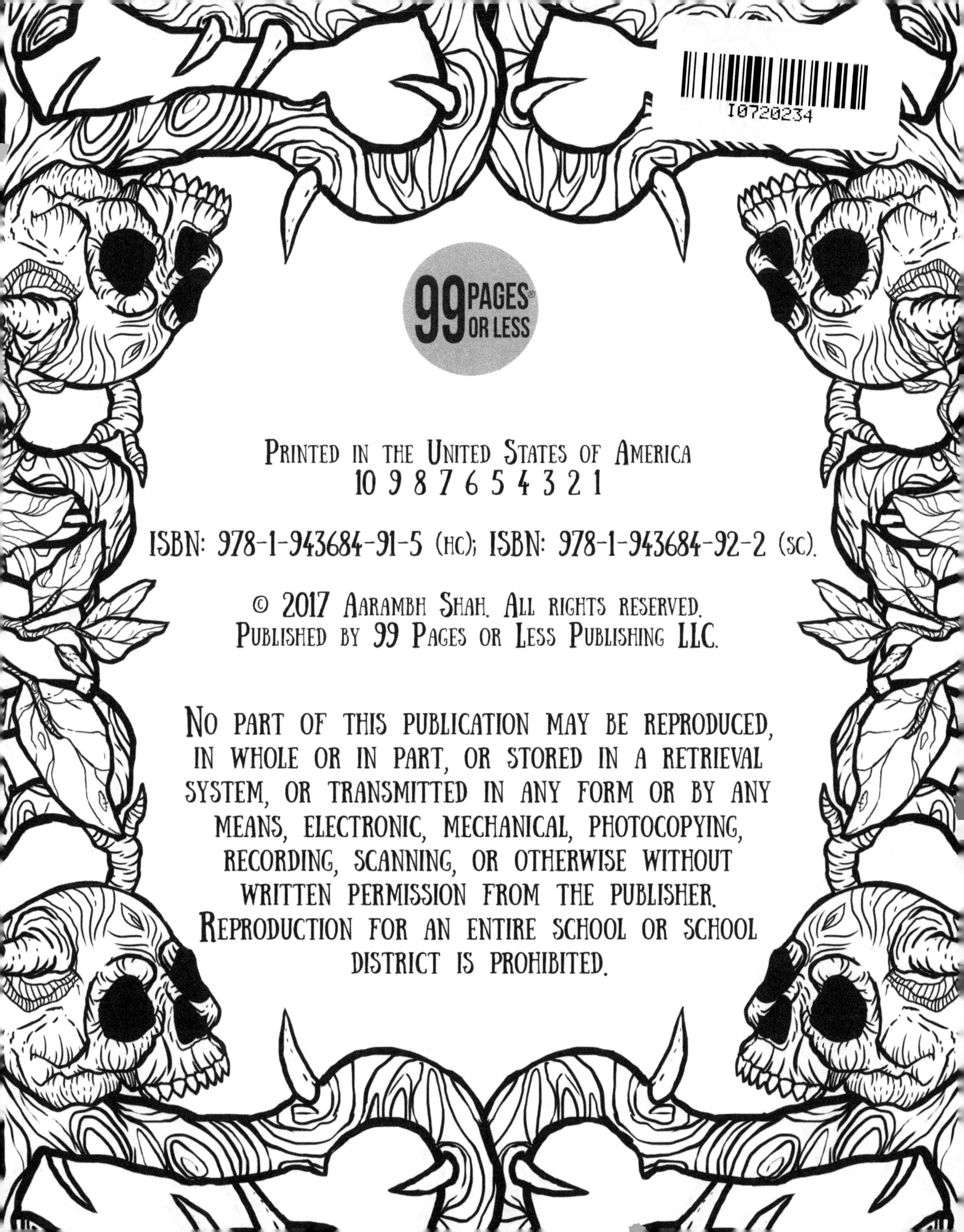

PRINTED IN THE UNITED STATES OF AMERICA
10 9 8 7 6 5 4 3 2 1

ISBN: 978-1-943684-91-5 (HC); ISBN: 978-1-943684-92-2 (SC).

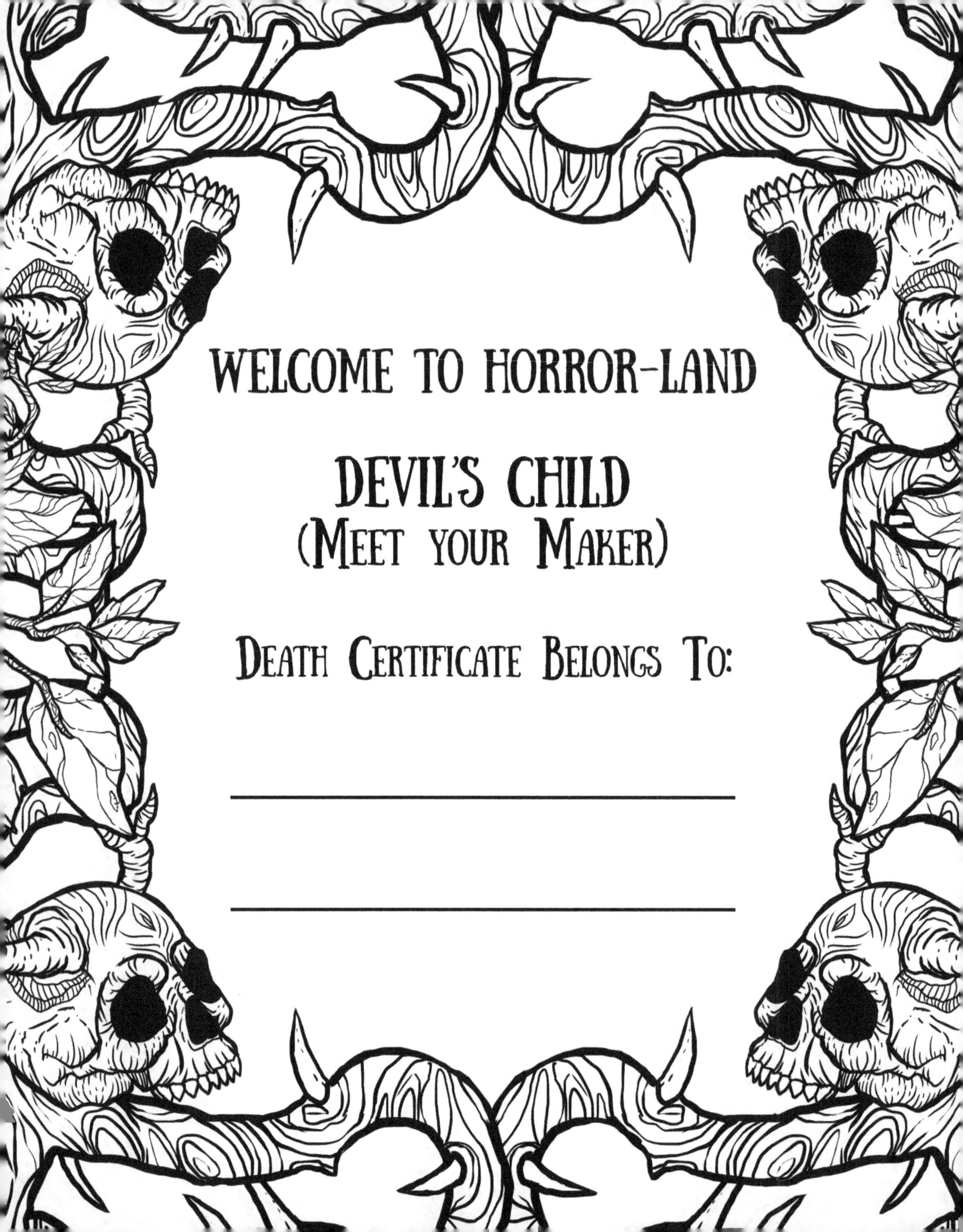

WELCOME TO HORROR-LAND

DEVIL'S CHILD
(MEET YOUR MAKER)

DEATH CERTIFICATE BELONGS TO:

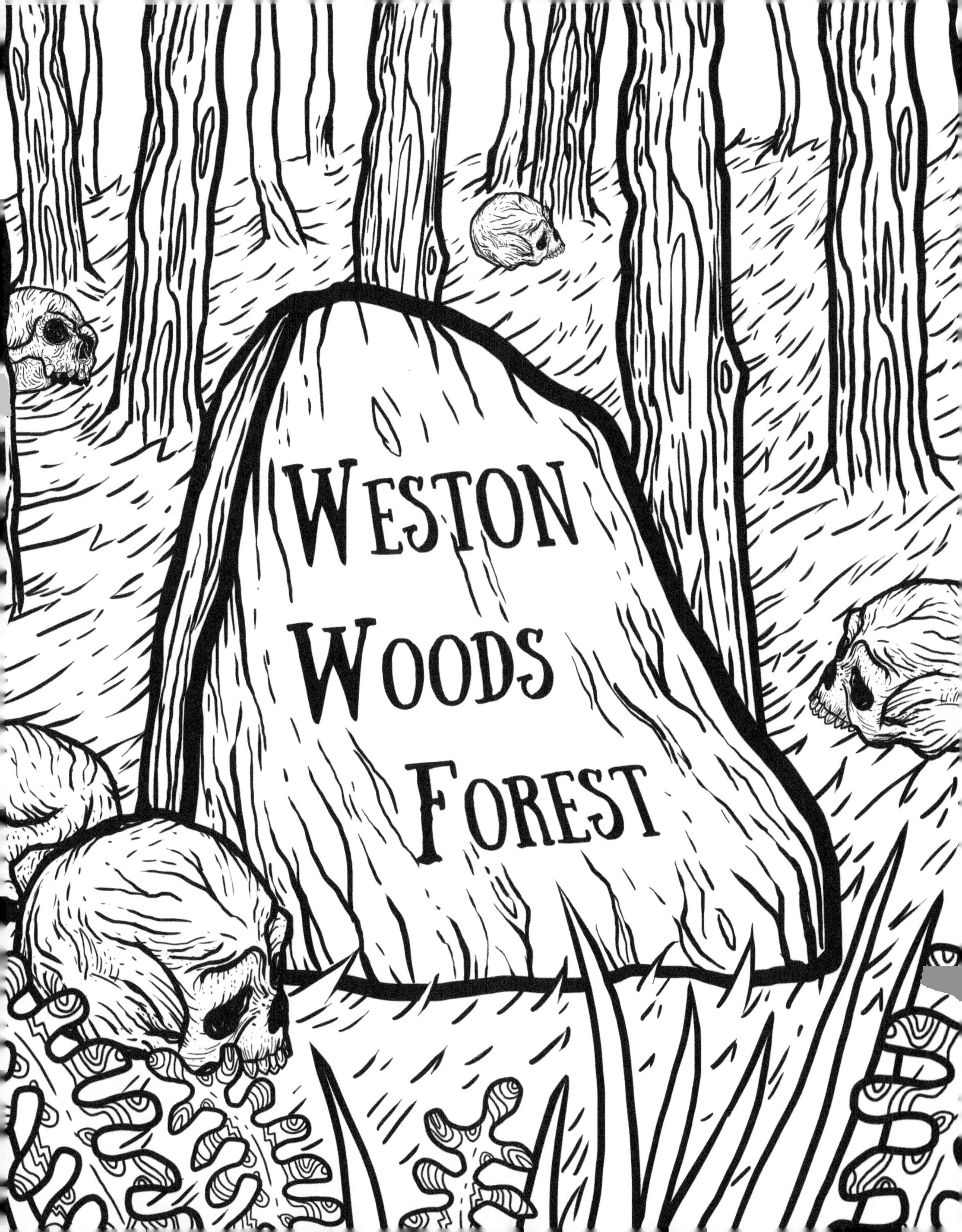

Weston
Woods
Forest

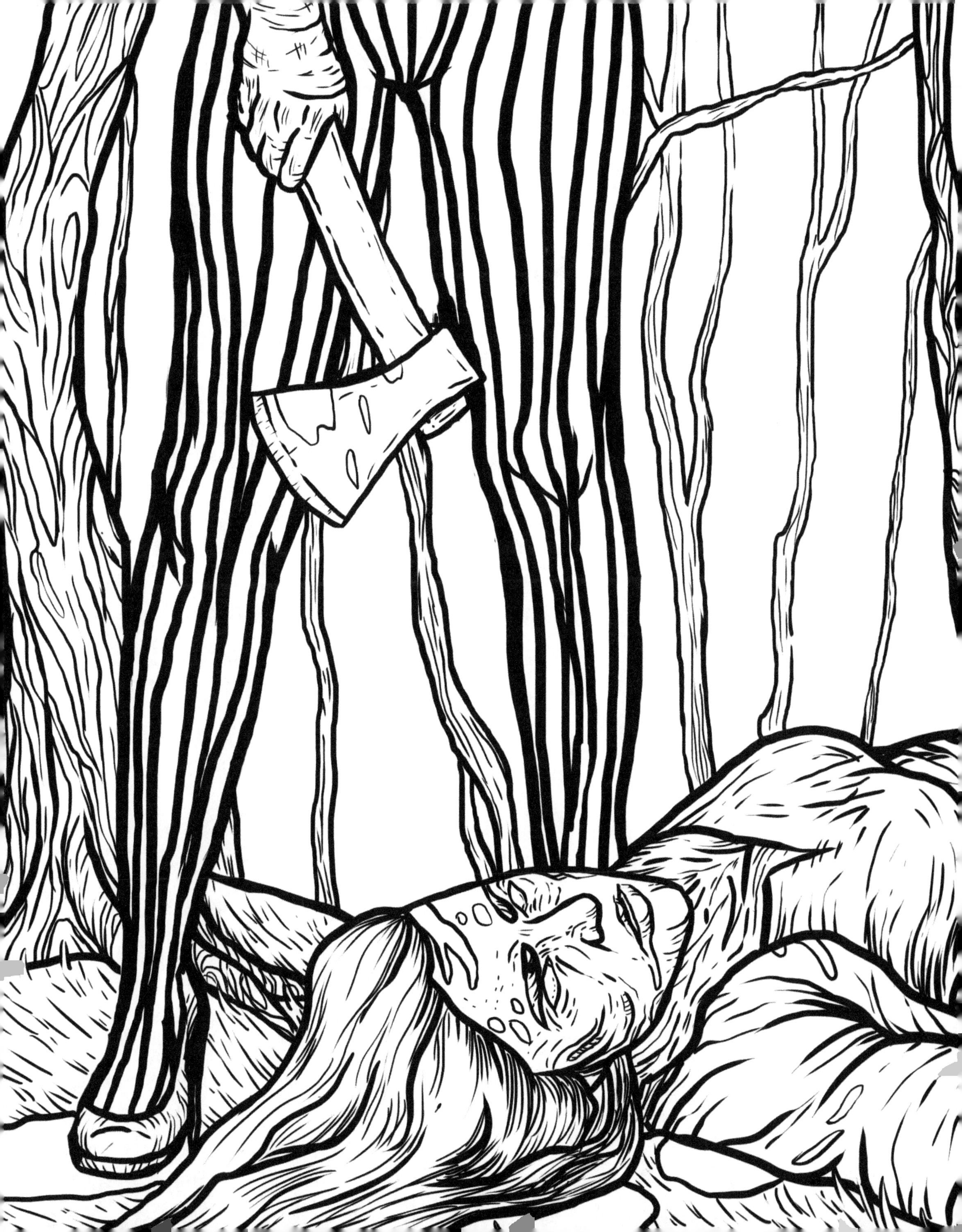

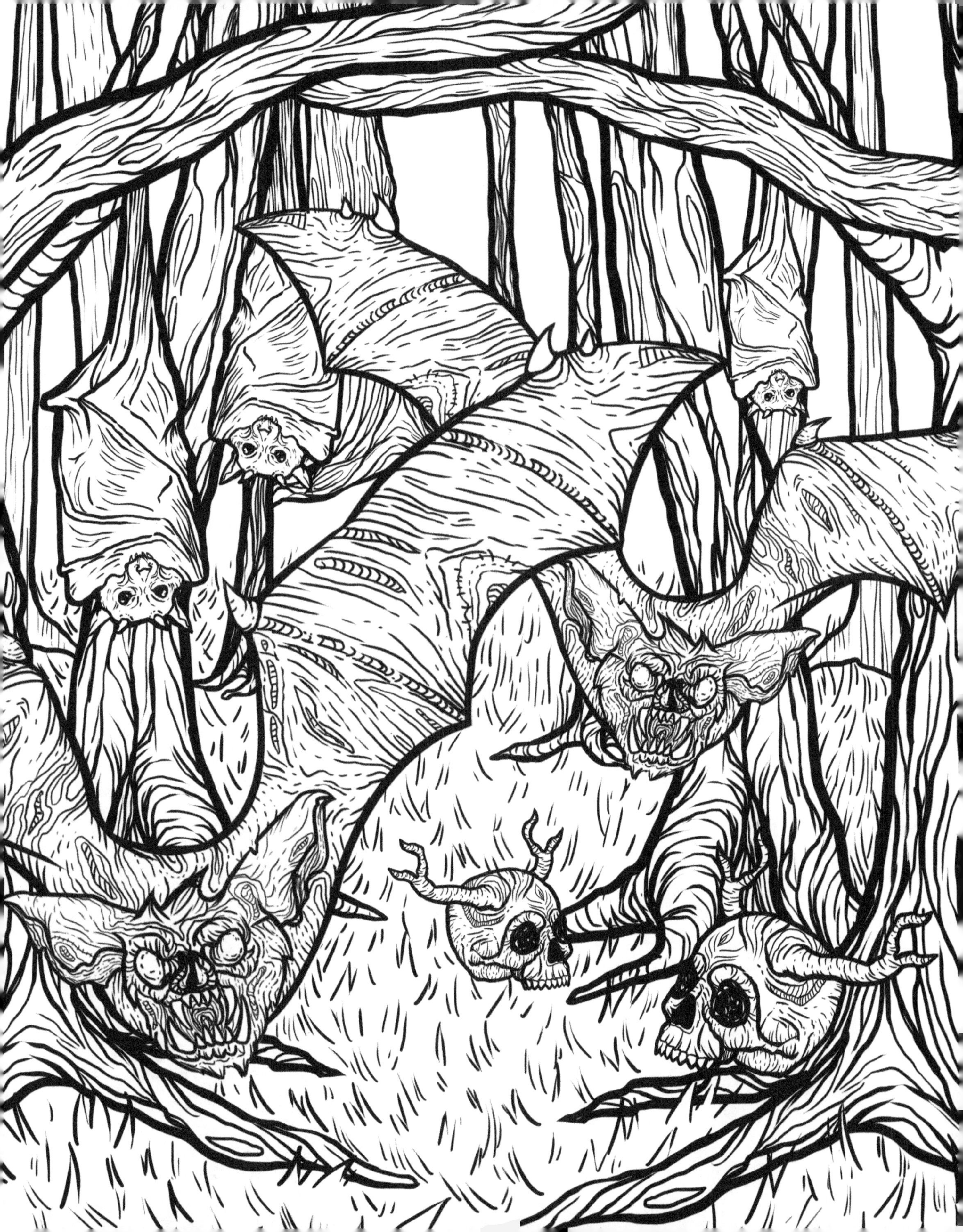

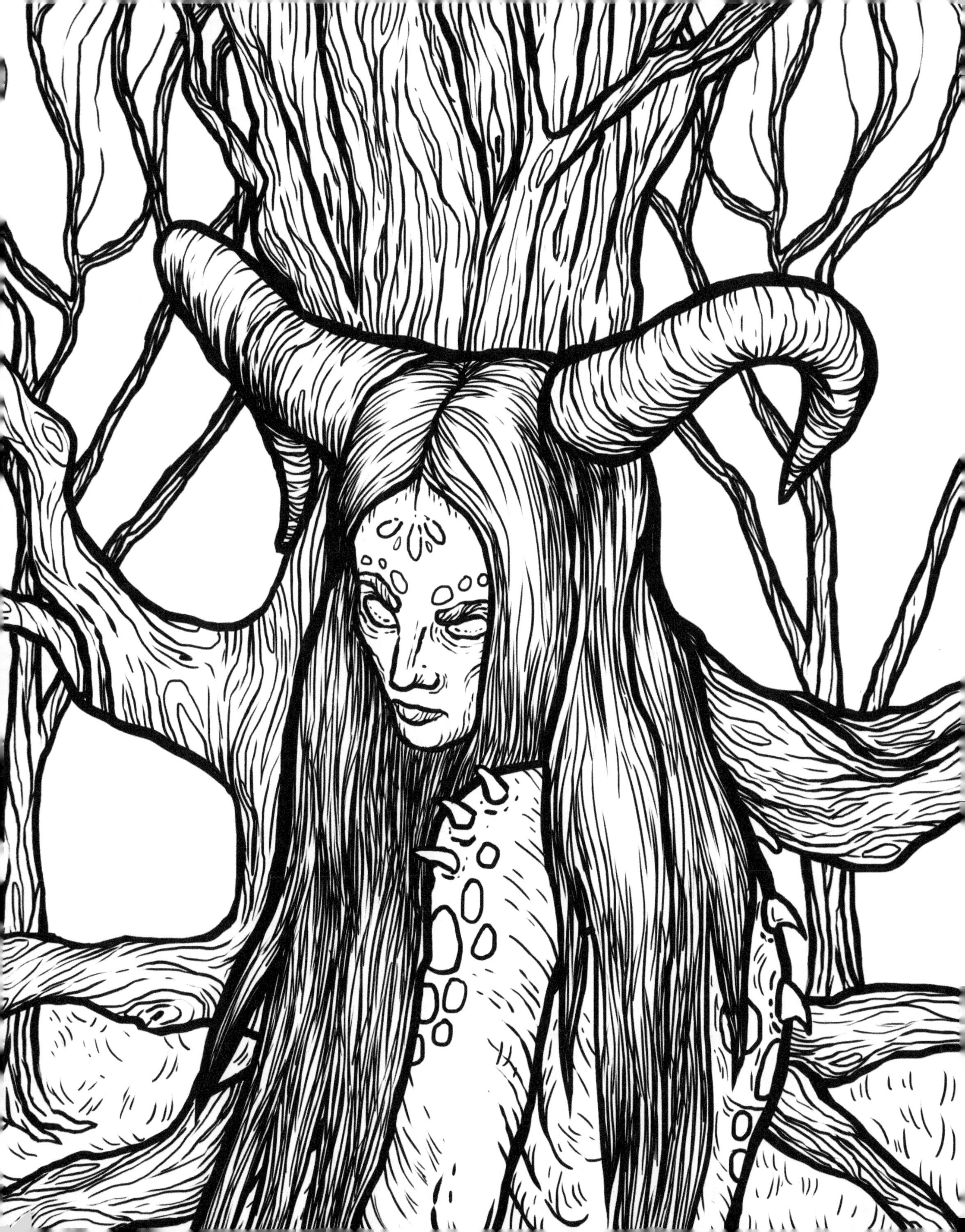

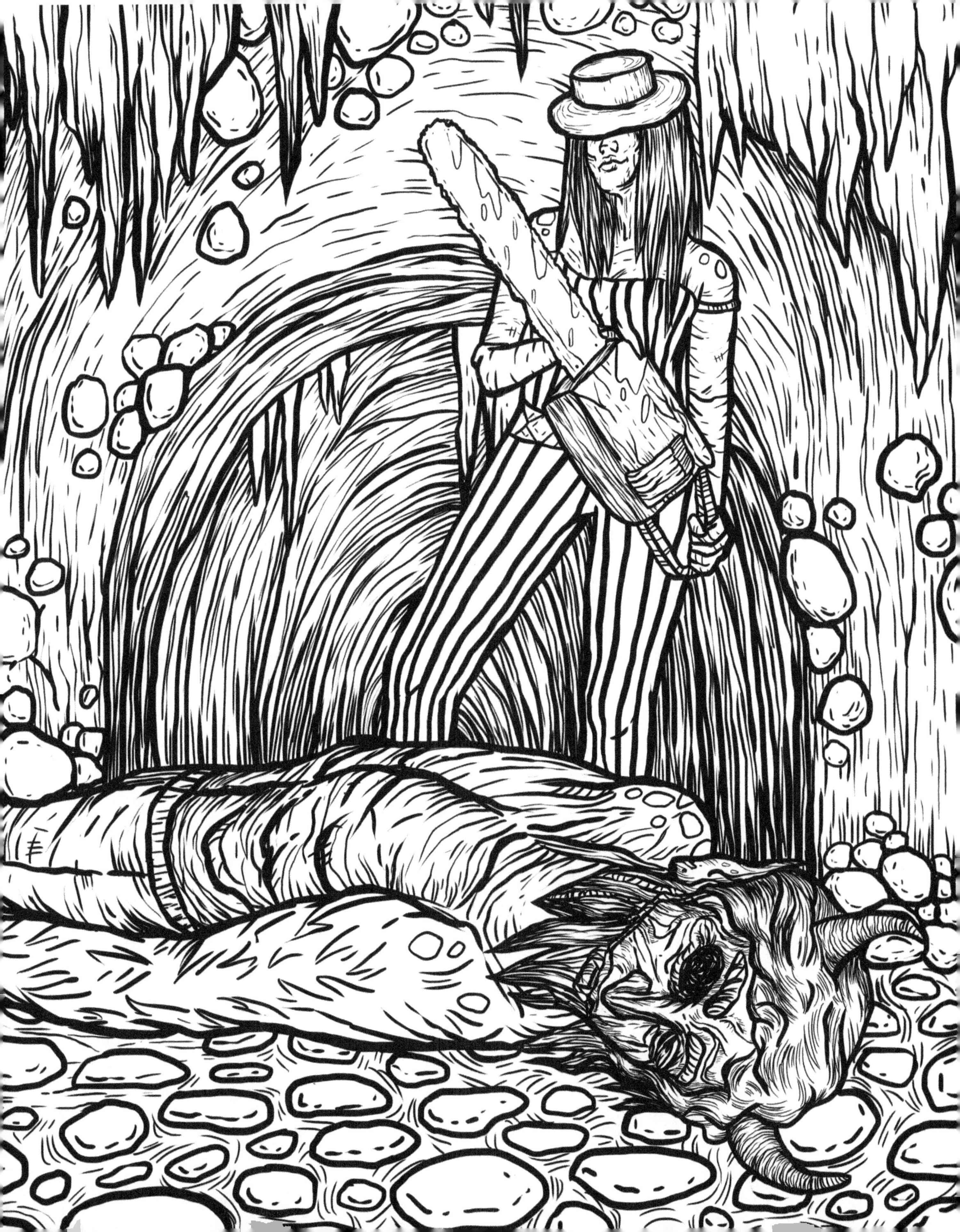

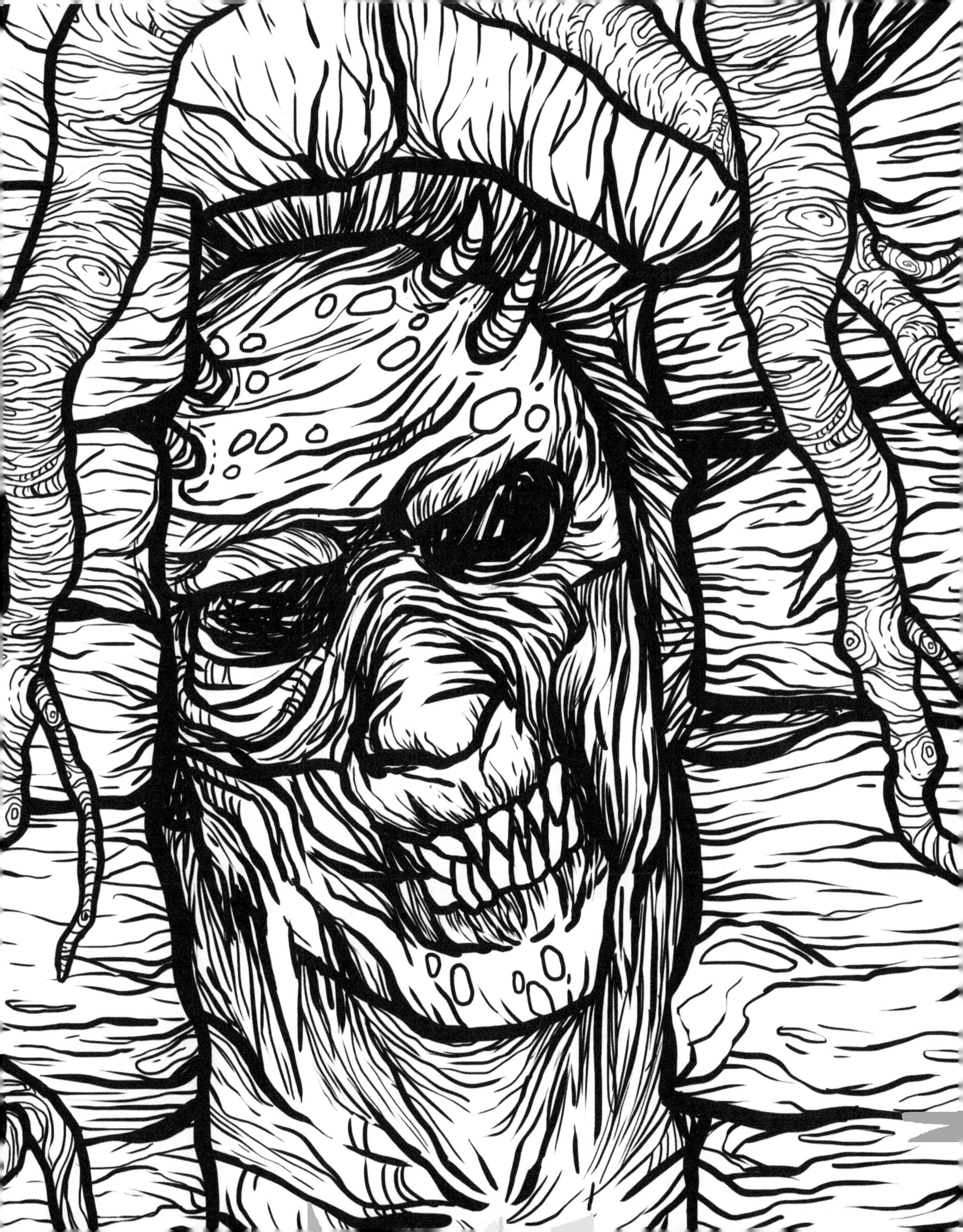

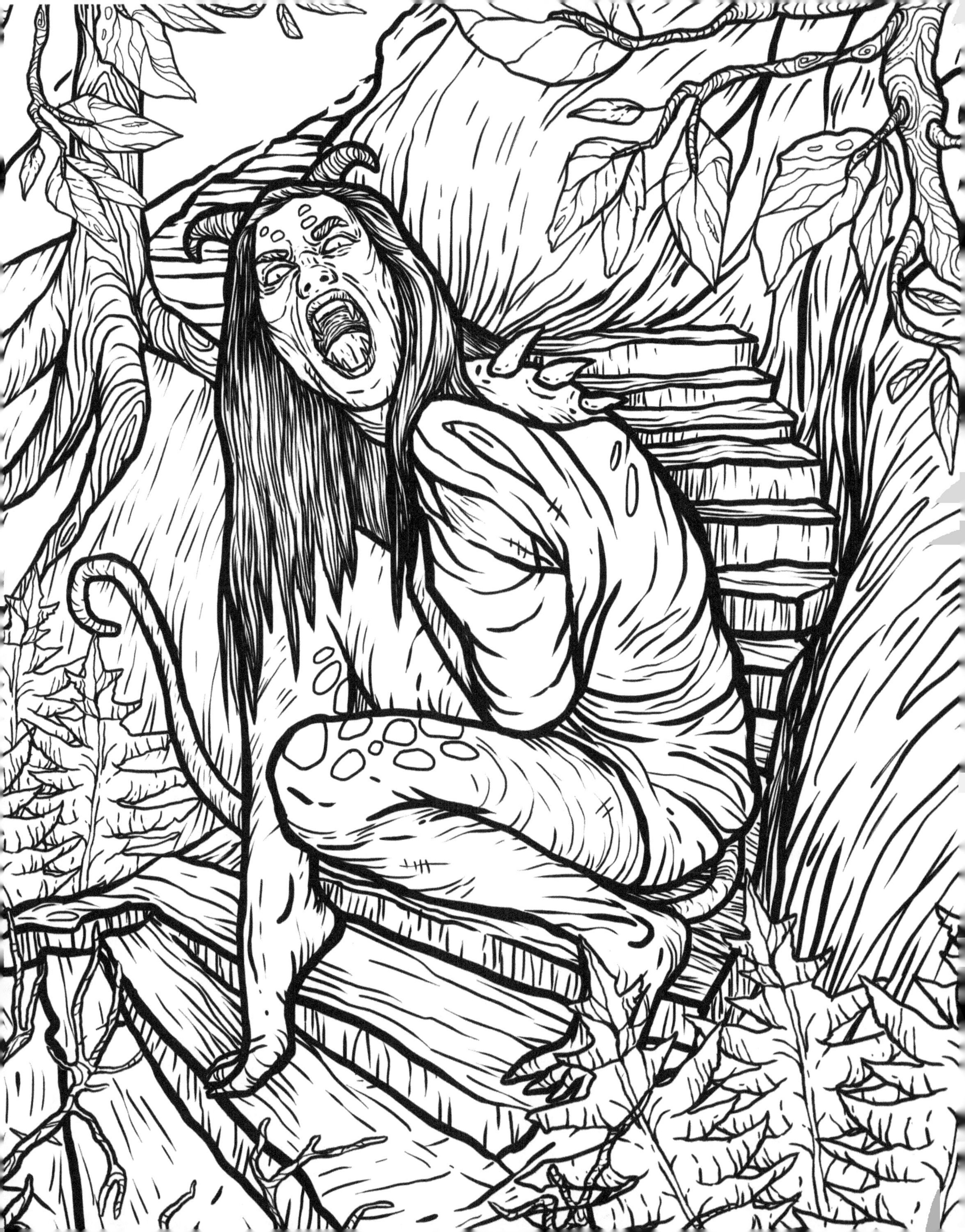

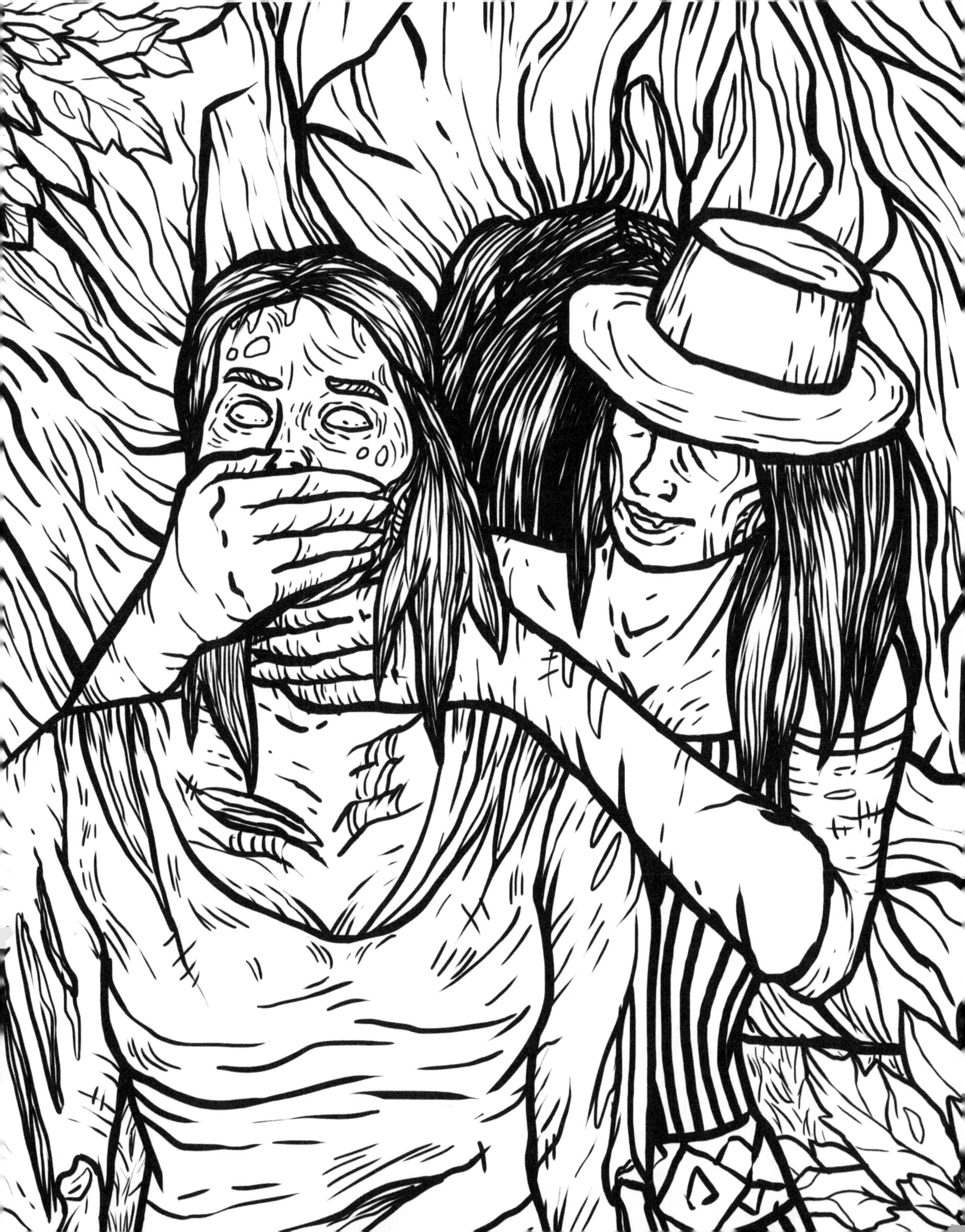

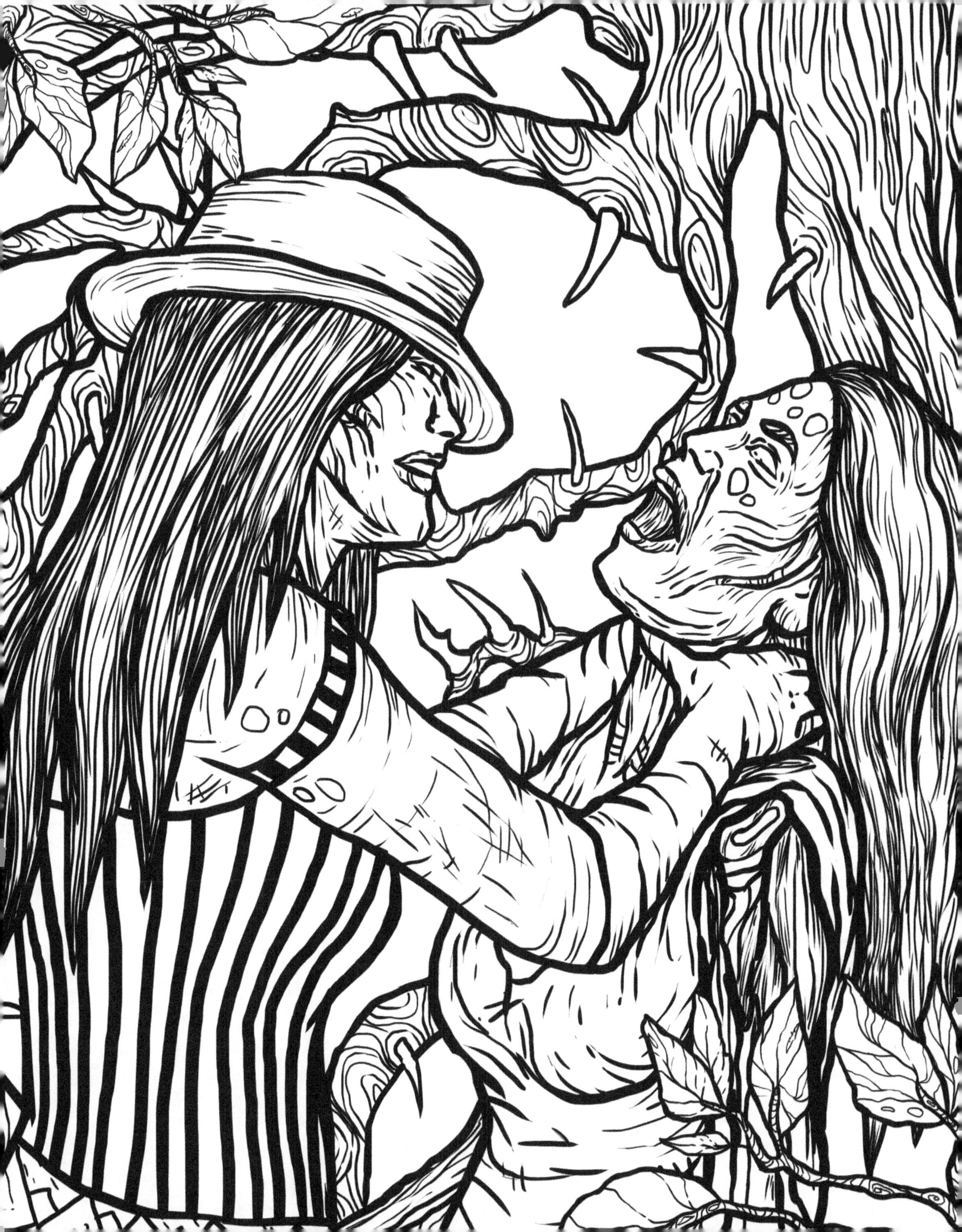

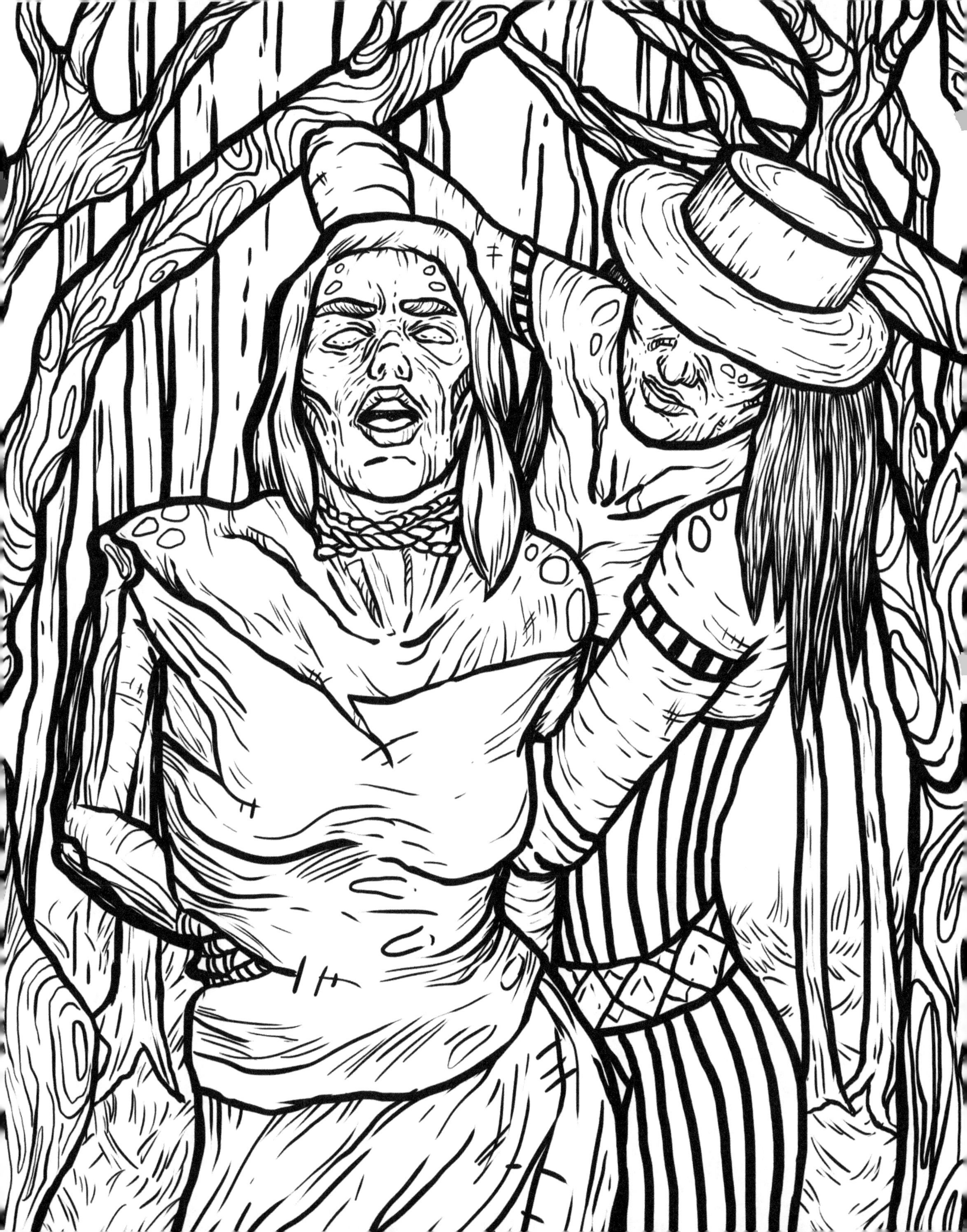

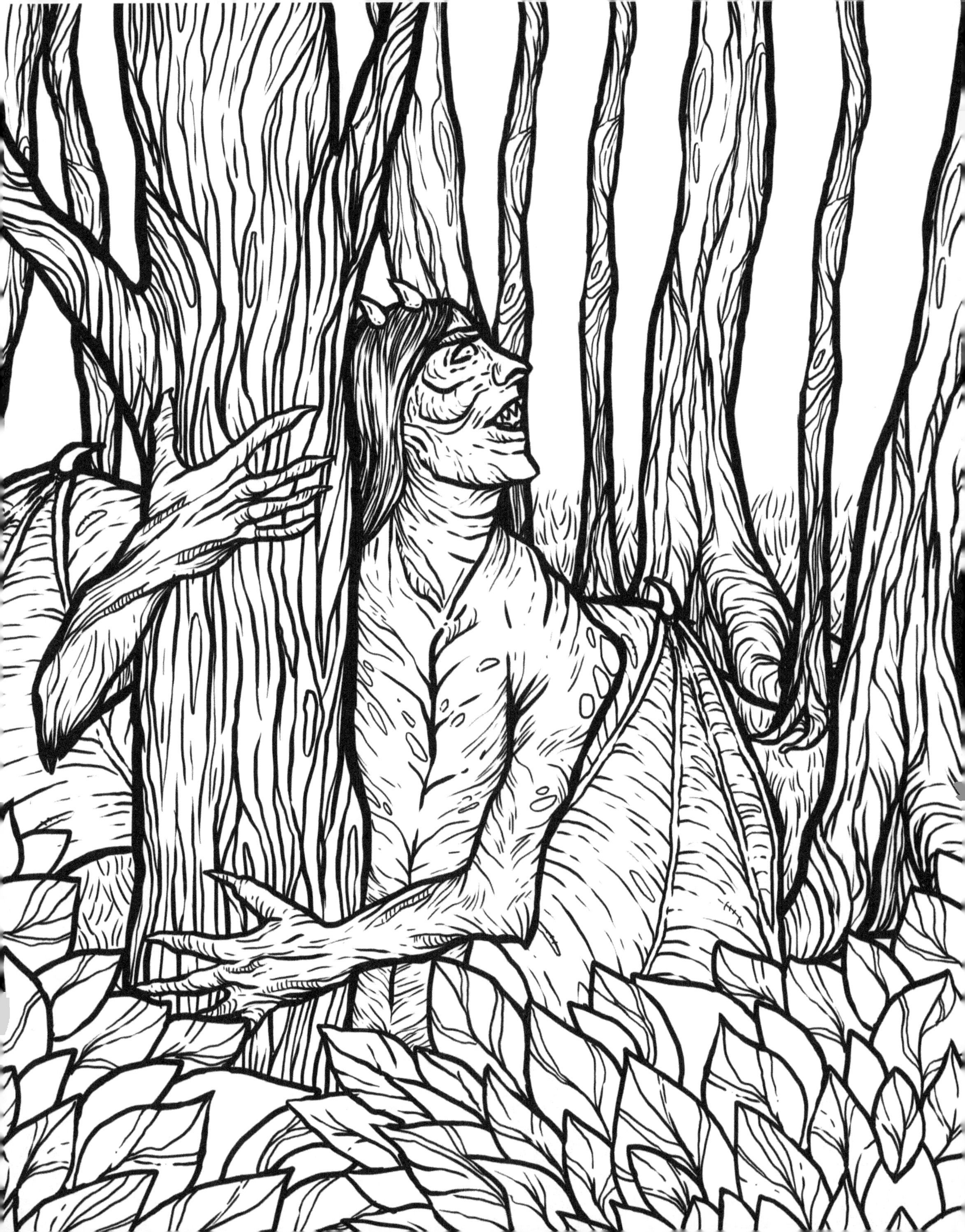

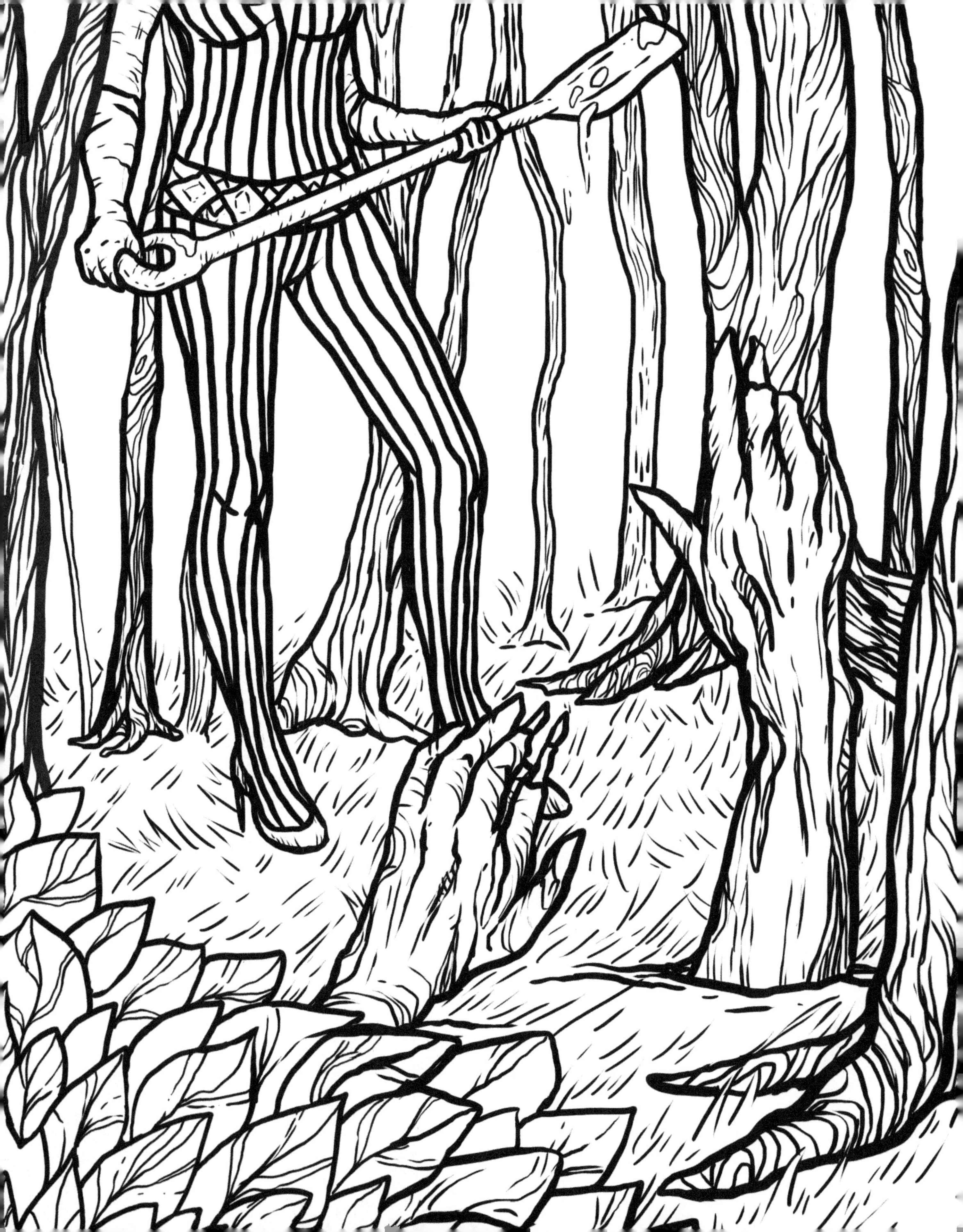

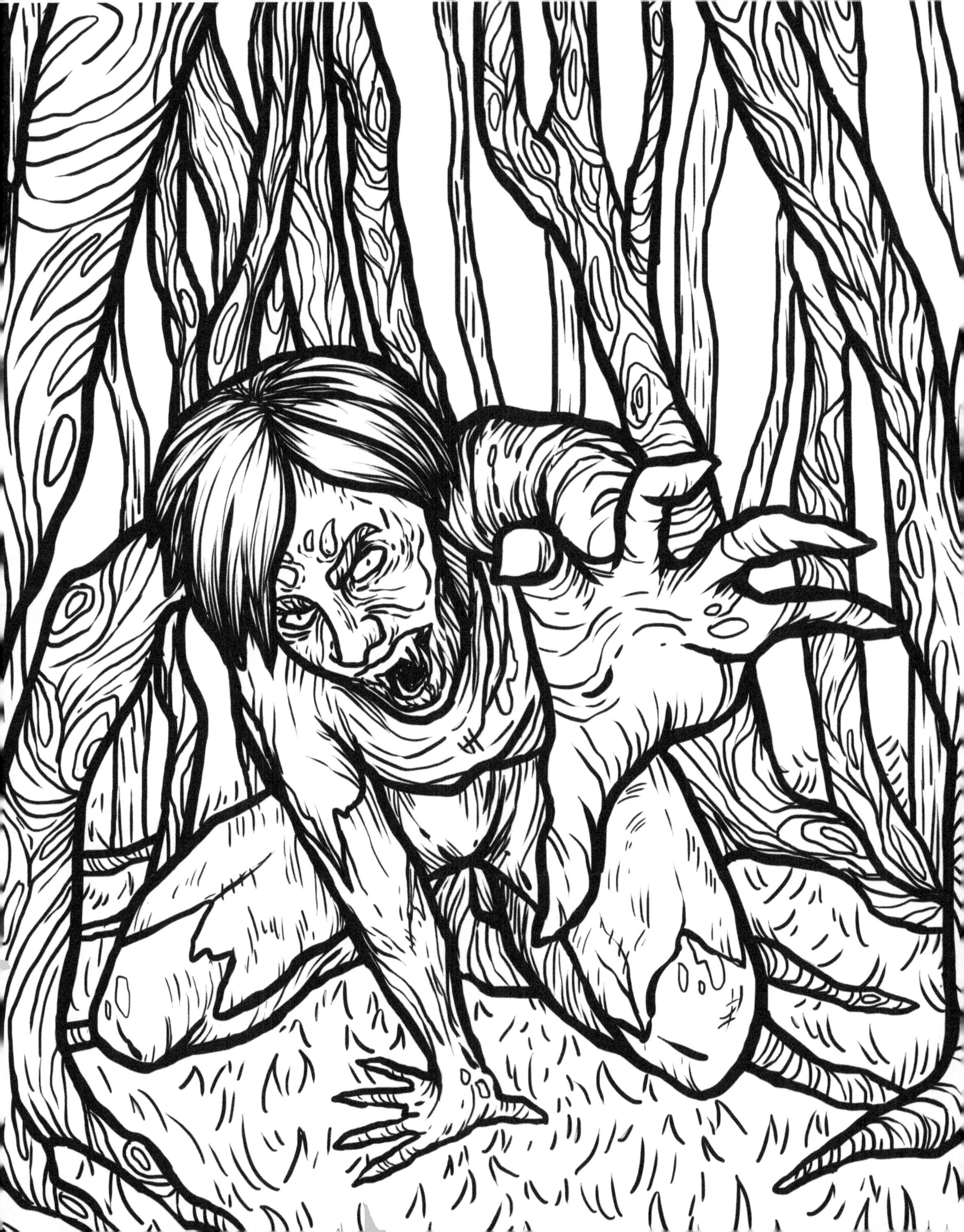

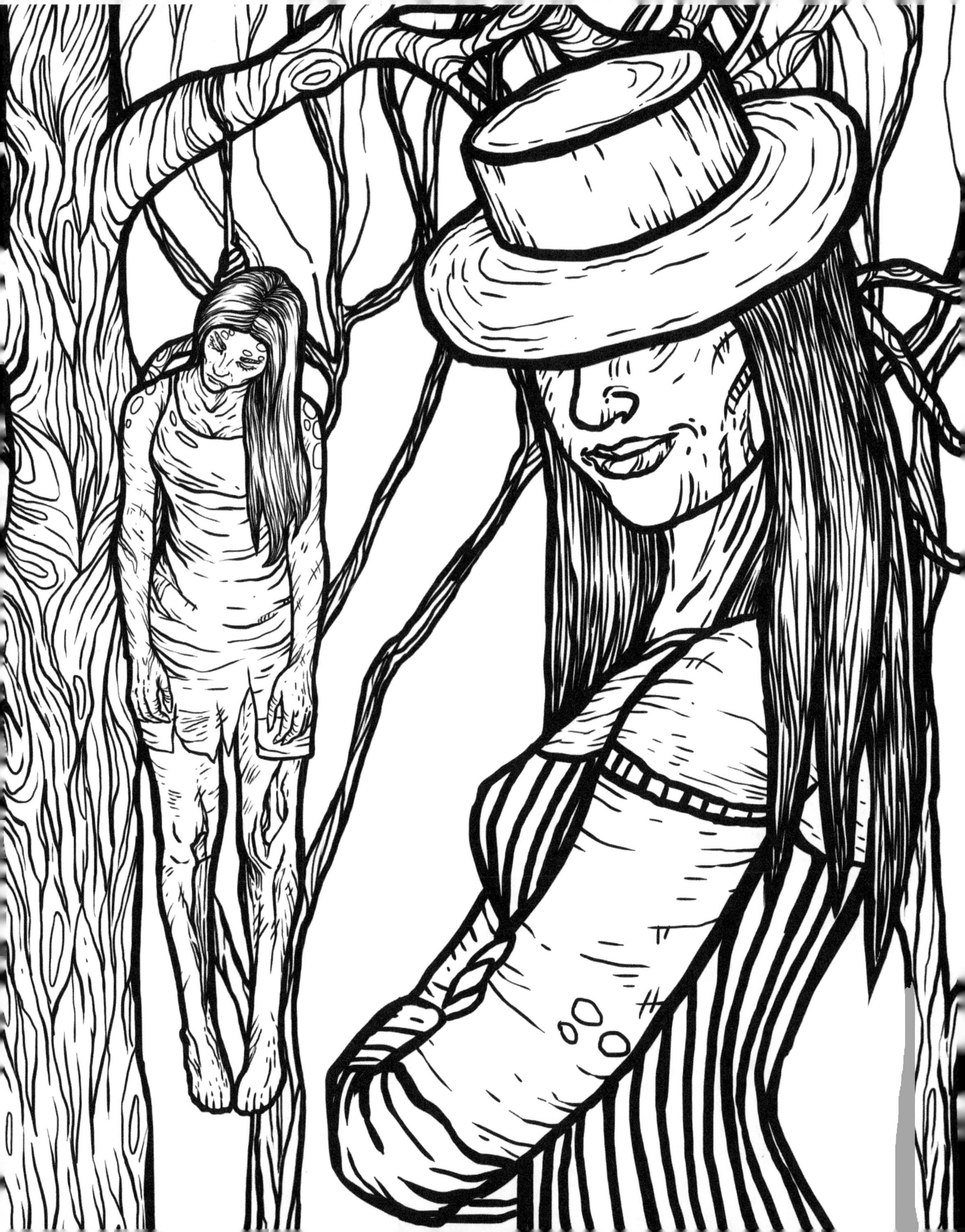

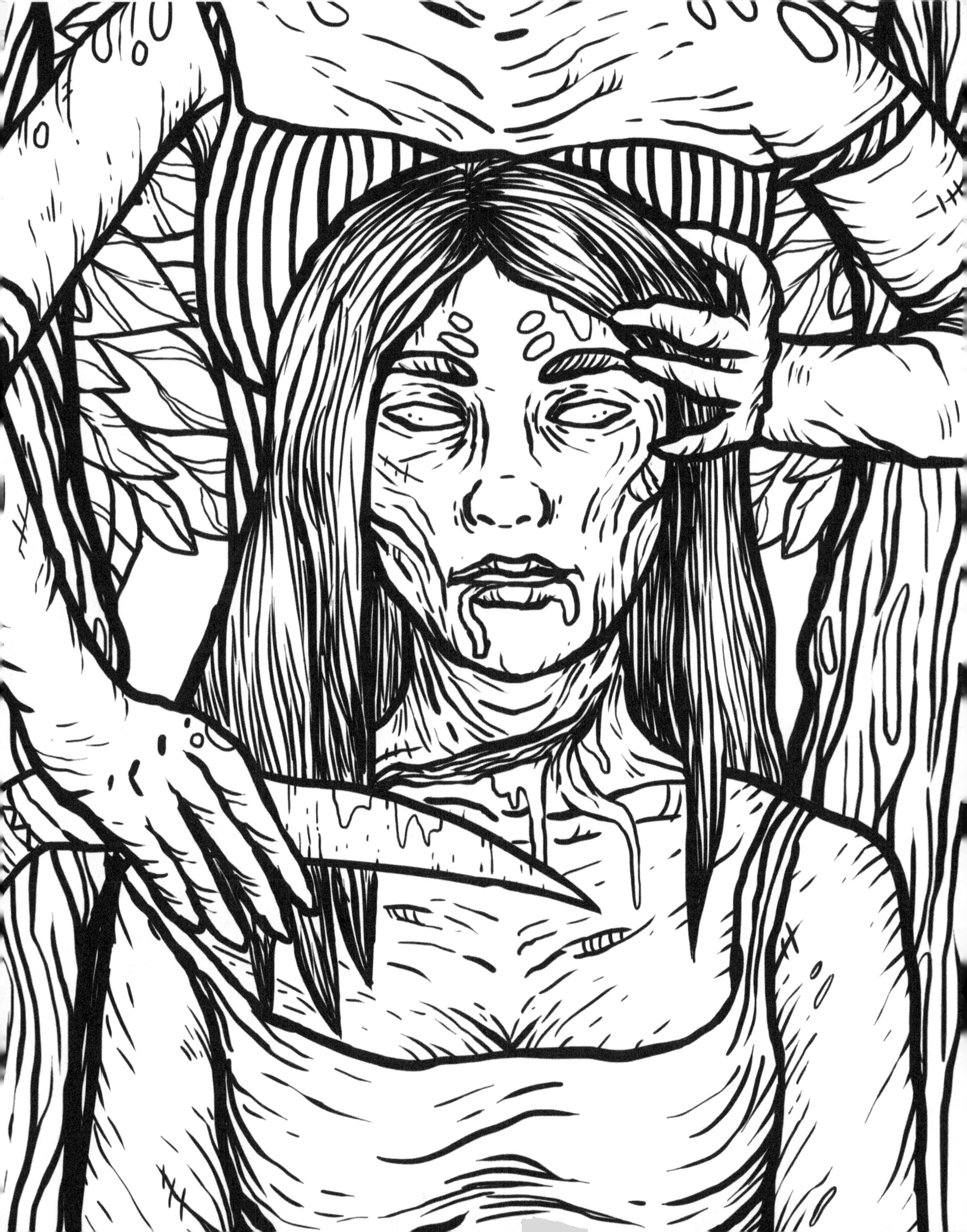

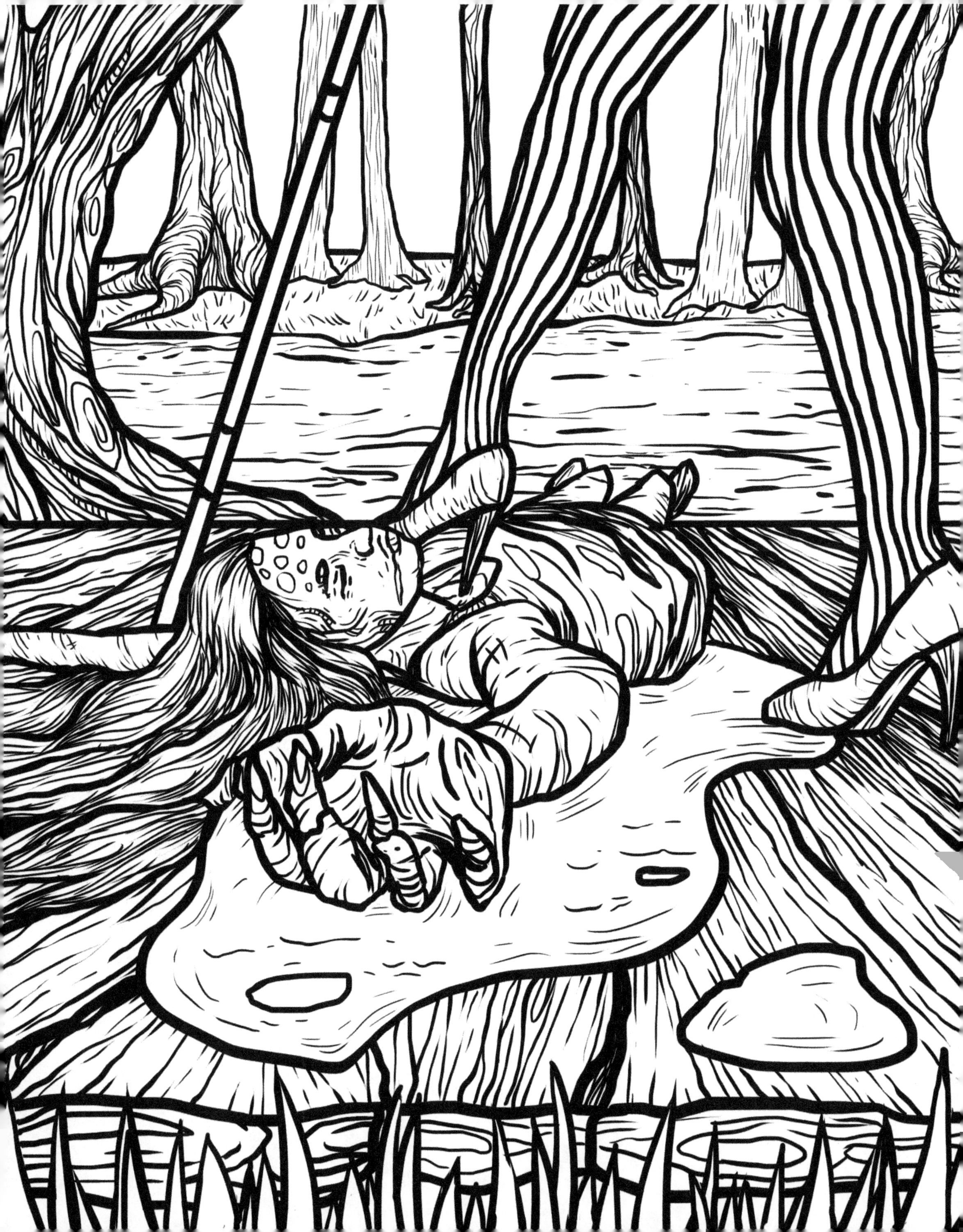

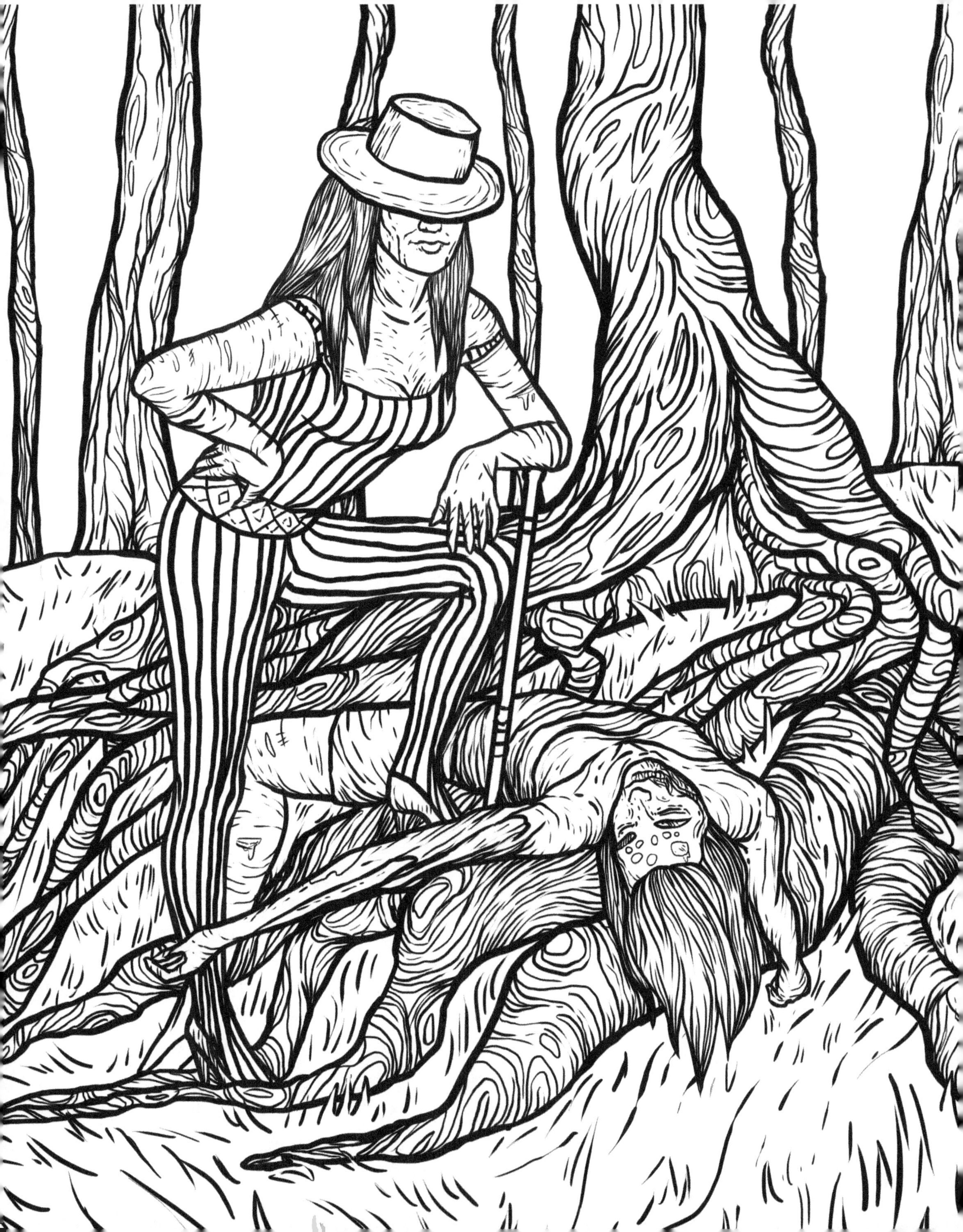

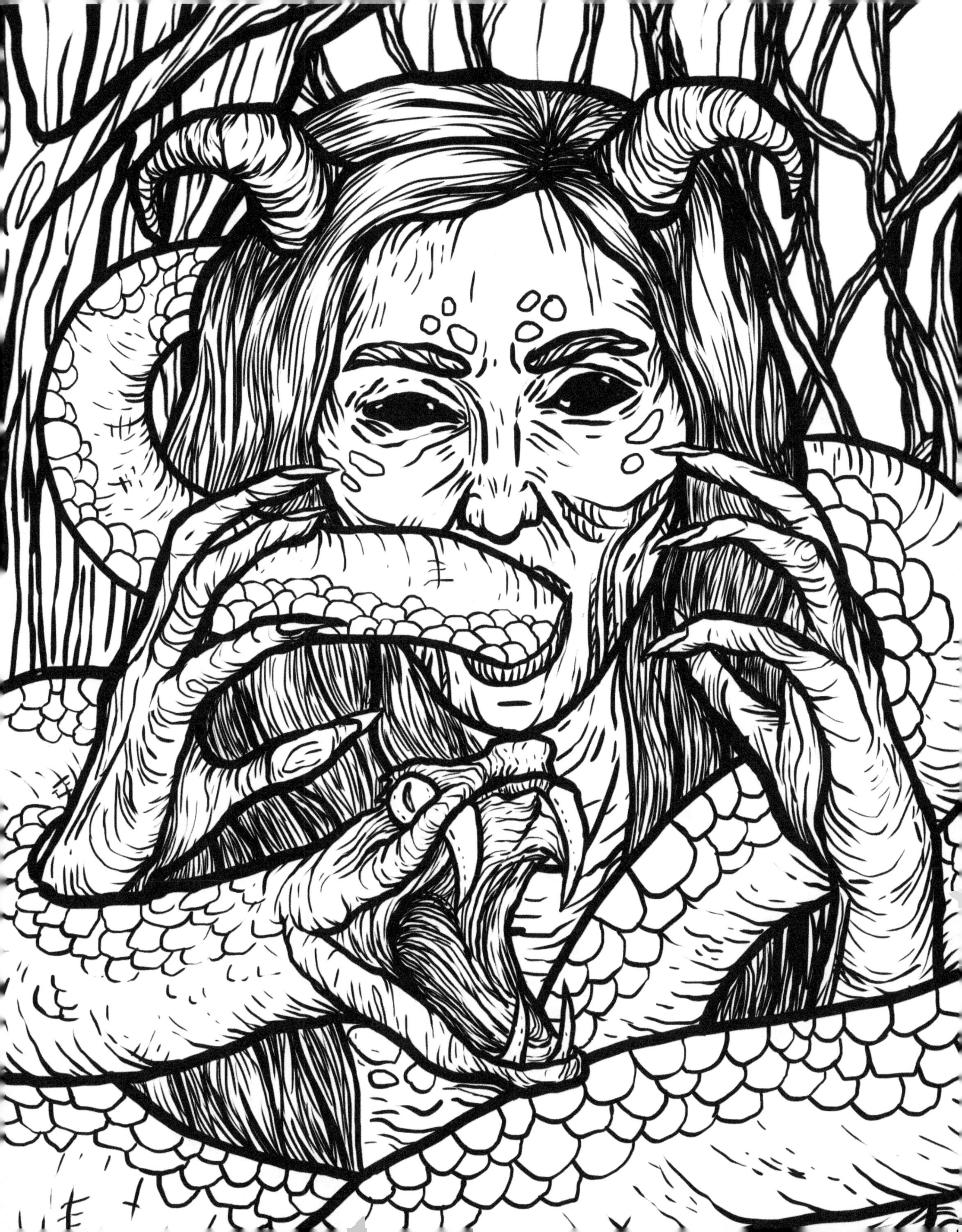

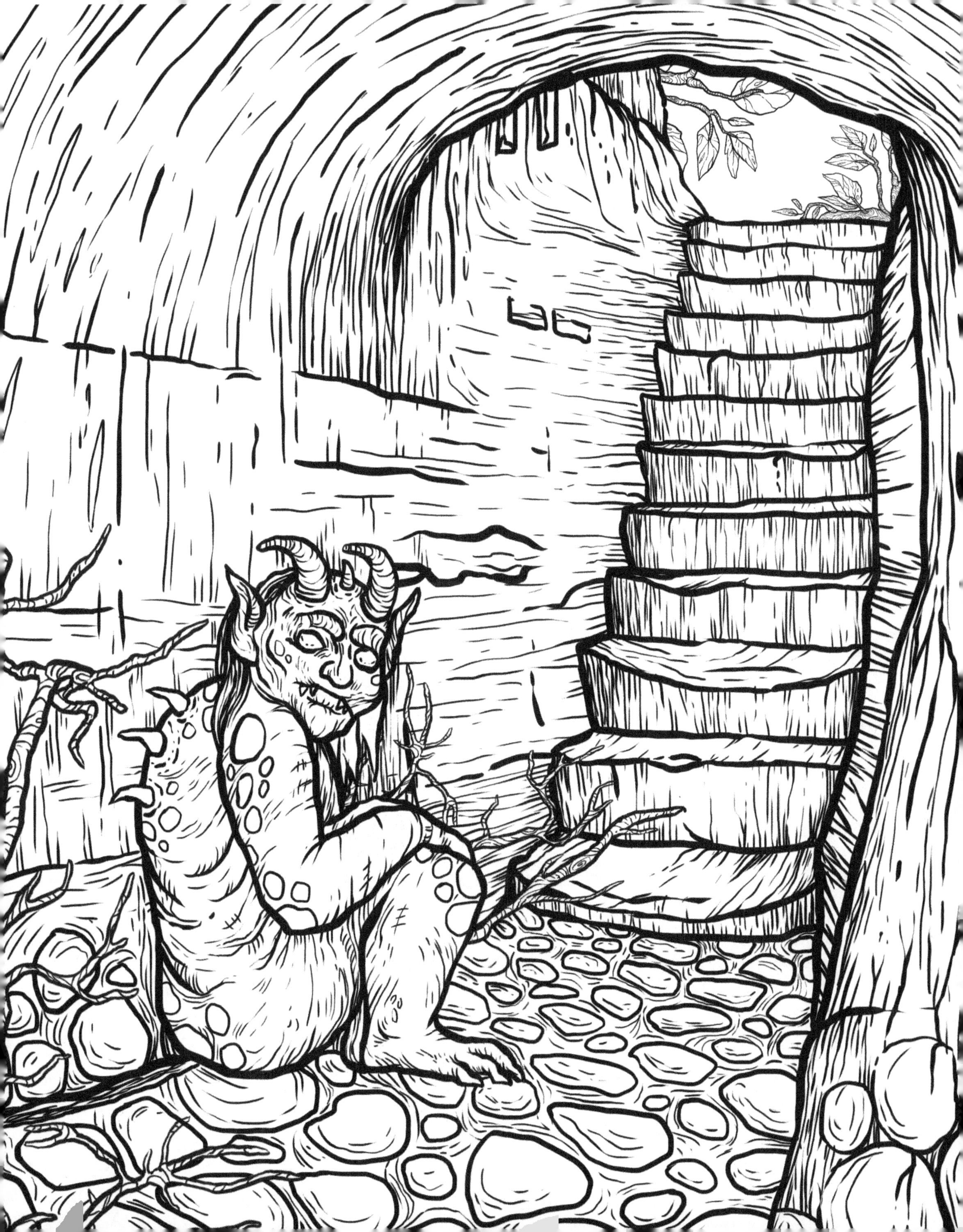

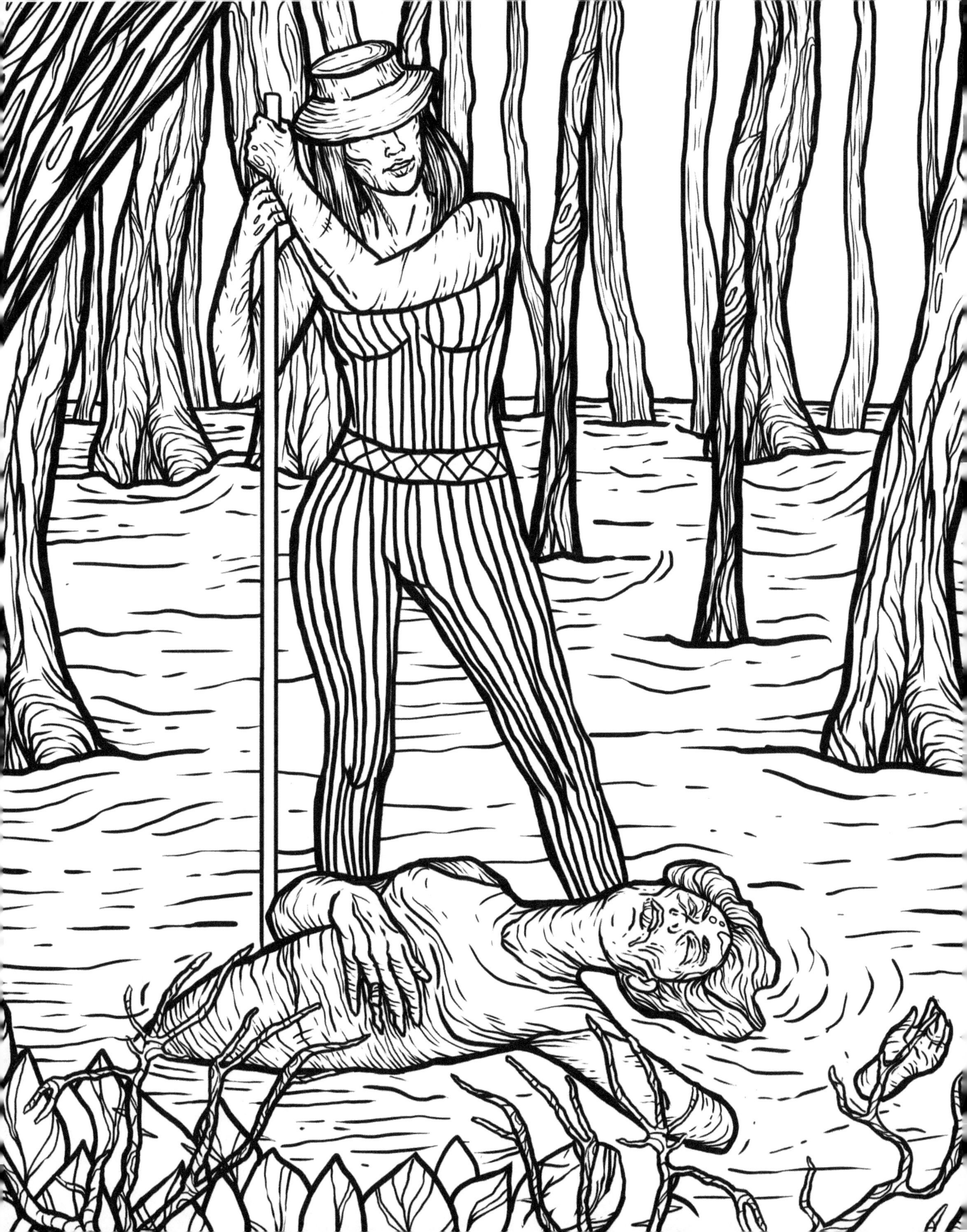

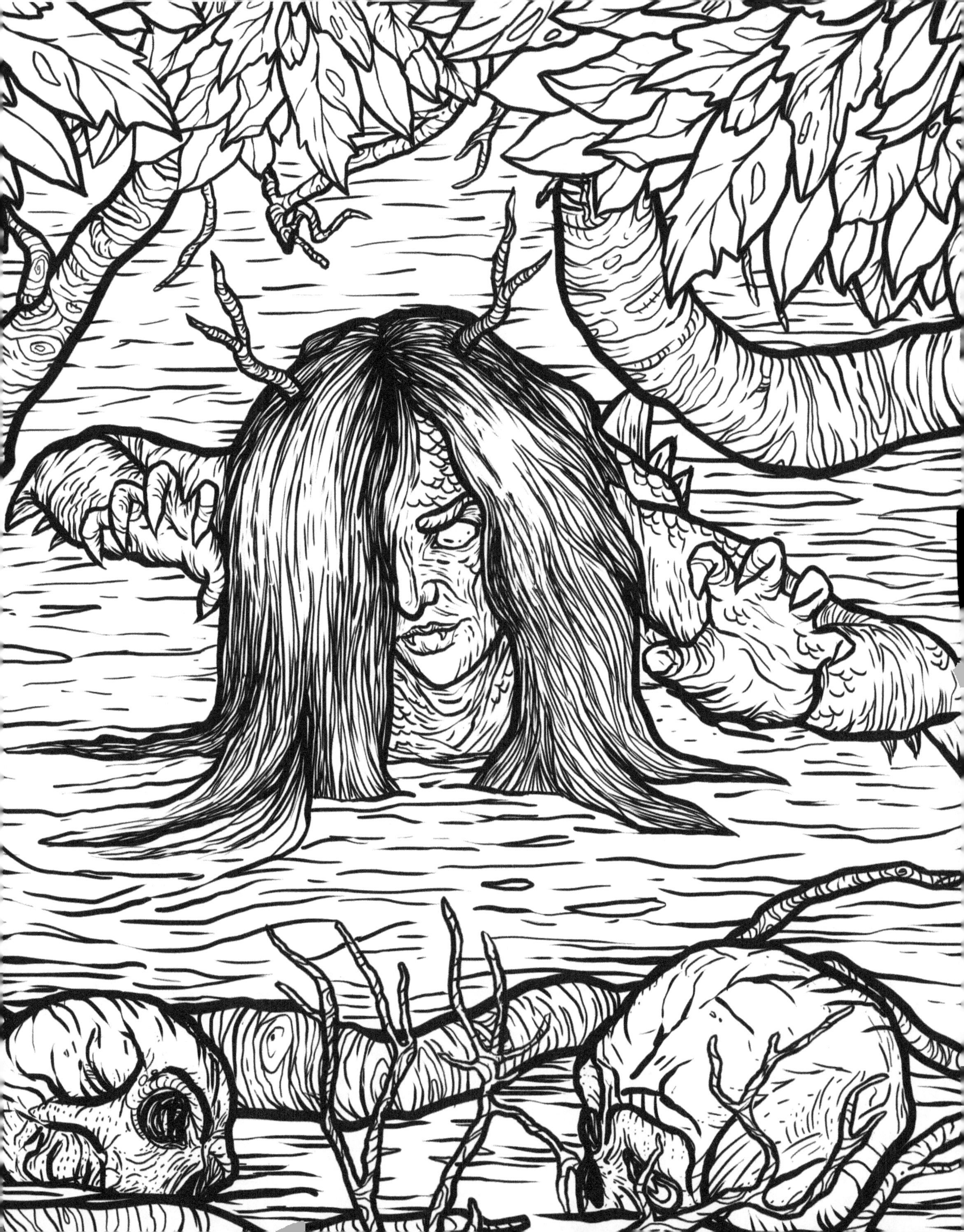

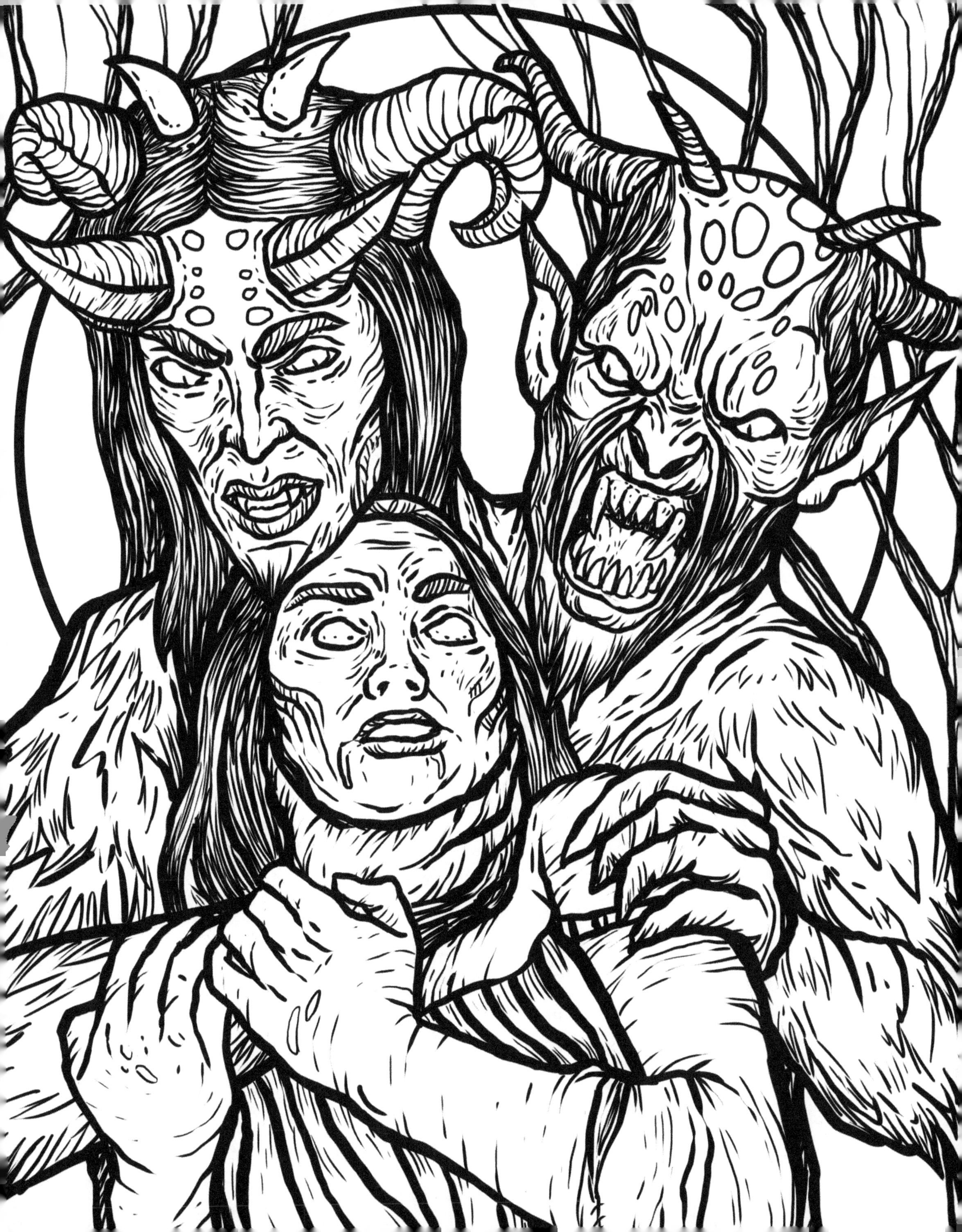